Scan the QR code
to read and listen to the
glossary words for FREE!

**glossary** - *Meanings of words.*

Dados Internacionais de Catalogação na Publicação (CIP) de acordo com ISBD

K57j Kipling, Rudyard
The jungle book - Easier Classics Reading / Rudyard Kipling. – Jandira : W. Books, 2025.
120 p. ; 12,8cm x 19,8cm. – (Easier Classics Reading Library Children's Collection)

ISBN: 978-65-5294-259-3

1. Literatura infantojuvenil. 2. Literatura Infantil. 3. Clássicos. 4. Aventura. 5. Imaginação. 6. Fantasia. I. Título. II. Série.

2025-609

CDD 028.5
CDU 82-93

**Elaborado por Vagner Rodolfo da Silva - CRB-8/9410**
**Índice para catálogo sistemático:**
1. Literatura infantojuvenil 028.5
2. Literatura infantojuvenil 82-93

Easier Classics
The Jungle Book



Original story by Rudyard Kipling.
Text based on the adaptation by Gemma Barder.
Illustrations by Archina Laezza.



1st edition in 2025
www.cirandacultural.com.br

# THE JUNGLE BOOK

Rudyard Kipling

W. Books

# Meet the Characters

Mowgli

Mother and Father Wolf

Grey

Shere Khan

Bagheera

Baloo

Kaa

Bandar

## Chapter 1

The Indian jungle was full of animals, big and small. But one of these **creatures** was different.

It walked on two legs and had no fur, feathers or scales.

It was a young, hungry boy who had lost his parents. He crawled inside a cave.

But he was not alone.

**creatures** - A living thing, that is not a plant, such as a human or an animal.

The cave was actually a wolf **den**. Inside were Mother Wolf, Father Wolf and their **cubs**.

'Look, a man **cub**,' said Father Wolf, stepping closer to the boy.

'Be careful!' said Mother Wolf. 'Humans don't treat animals very well.'

'It is too young to hurt us,' said Father Wolf.

**den** - The home of a wild animal, often a cave or a tunnel underground.

**cubs** - Baby wild animals such as wolves or bears.

Mother Wolf carefully walked towards the man cub. She licked him, making him giggle.

**Suddenly**, Father Wolf began to growl because Shere Khan, an evil tiger, stood outside the cave.

'The man cub is mine,' said Shere Khan. 'Hand him over.'

Mother Wolf growled. She wanted to **protect** the boy.

**Suddenly** - Quickly and not expected to happen.

**protect** - To look after.

Mother Wolf and Father Wolf stepped out of the cave.

Shere Khan smiled. He knew that they couldn't protect the boy without the wolf **leader**, Akela's, **permission**.

'Akela will meet the boy tomorrow at the **council** of wolves,' said Father Wolf.

'If he isn't accepted, he is mine,' said Shere Khan, walking away.

**leader** - The person or animal in charge of a group.

**permission** - To let someone do something.

**council** - A group that meets at planned times to make decisions.

## Chapter 2

'We'll name the boy Mowgli,' said Mother Wolf. 'We'll raise him like one of our cubs.'

'Remember, he's not a wolf. He's a man,' Father Wolf said. 'Men kill animals like us.'

'We can't give him to Shere Khan. He hates humans and will hurt the boy,' said Mother Wolf.

The next night, Akela sat on Council Rock, a place above the jungle, where the animals had meetings.

The animals moved away as

Shere Khan joined the meeting.

Father Wolf wanted Mowgli to

join the wolf pack to be protected.

But Shere Khan hated humans

and thought Mowgli would kill

the animals when he grew older.

'To be protected by the pack, two animals who are not his mother and father must help to teach the boy the **laws of the jungle**,' said Akela.

'I can help,' said Bagheera, the panther. 'I know how men think. I can teach him as he grows.'

'Me too!' said Baloo, the brown bear.

**laws of the jungle** - The rules which the animals of the jungle follow.

'It is decided!' said Akela, loudly. 'The man cub has the protection of the pack!'

Mother Wolf **sighed with relief**.

'This is not the end,' said Shere Khan. 'The man cub will be mine!'

**sighed with relief** - *To relax because something you were worried or frightened about is not a problem anymore.*

## Chapter 3

As Mowgli grew older, Bagheera and Baloo taught him the laws of the jungle.

One morning, Bagheera and Baloo wanted to teach Mowgli the Master Words. The Master Words would let Mowgli talk to and understand every animal in the jungle.

But Mowgli wanted to play with his wolf brother, Grey, instead.

'Grey, Mowgli has work to do. Leave him be,' Bagheera said.

As Grey walked back to the wolf den, Mowgli **sighed in defeat**.

Slowly, they went through all of the Master Words. But Mowgli started to feel tired.

'One more time,' Bagheera ordered.

**sighed in defeat** - When someone breathes out for a long time because they have given up.

'Why do *I* have lessons all the time?' Mowgli asked.

'Because Shere Khan has killed many humans before, so you may need to ask others for help,' Bagheera warned.

Mowgli thought he could be brave and fight Shere Khan instead.

'It's not fair!' shouted Mowgli, running away.

## Chapter 4

Mowgli ran and ran.

He knew that Bagheera and Baloo were only trying to help him. But he just wanted to be like everyone else.

Mowgli stopped to sit under a tree.

Suddenly, something grabbed his arm. A group of monkeys pulled his arms and lifted him up into the trees.

'Let me go!' Mowgli shouted.

The monkeys didn't listen and laughed as they carried Mowgli further into the jungle.

Then, Mowgli saw Rann, the **kite**, flying high above. The bird was **wise** and might help him.

But Mowgli had never spoken to a bird before.

Mowgli called to Rann using the Master Words.

Rann flew down and watched the monkeys carrying Mowgli. She nodded her head and flew off.

**kite** - *A type of bird.*

**wise** - *When someone is very smart.*

Far away, Baloo and Bagheera were wondering where Mowgli was.

Rann, the kite, flew down and called to them.

'Monkeys took the man cub to the **ancient ruins**,' said Rann.

Bagheera and Baloo ran off into the jungle to find Mowgli.

**ancient ruins** - A really old building that has fallen down over time.

## Chapter 5

Mowgli sat in the ancient ruins. Monkeys of every size pulled his hair and poked his skin.

Then, a large monkey **appeared**. It was the largest monkey Mowgli had ever seen.

'Man cub!' the large monkey said, loudly. 'We have wanted you to join us for so long!'

**appeared** - When something is seen that wasn't there before.

'Take me back!' Mowgli shouted.

The large monkey laughed, making the other monkeys laugh too.

'But why would you want to leave?' asked the large monkey. 'We want you to come and live with us.'

'My name is Bandar,' said the large monkey. 'We need your help.'

'Why do you need my help?' asked Mowgli.

'You're a human,' said Bandar. 'You must stay with us and teach us everything you know.'

'We want to know how to build houses and make clothes,' Bandar **explained**. 'But most of all, we want to make fire!'

'But I don't know how to do any of those things!' Mowgli said.

Bandar stepped closer to Mowgli and said, angrily, 'Then you had better learn.'

Mowgli was scared.

**explained** - To help someone understand something.

Bagheera and Baloo ran through the jungle towards the ancient ruins.

As they reached the river, Bagheera suddenly stopped.

'What are you doing?' Baloo asked.

'We need Kaa,' Bagheera answered. 'Kaa is the only creature that Bandar is afraid of.'

'I'm not going near that snake!' said Baloo.

'Kaa won't eat us if we tell her there is a whole **troop** of monkeys she can eat for helping us,' said Bagheera.

Bagheera and Baloo found Kaa and asked her for help.

**troop** - *A group of monkeys.*

'Why should I help you?' Kaa said.

'Bandar is afraid of you,' Bagheera said. 'If you help us, you can eat all of the monkeys you want. We just want Mowgli.'

'I ssssuppose I could help,' she answered.

'Thank you,' Bagheera said, before leading everyone to the ruins.

When they arrived at the ancient ruins, Baloo climbed on to a fallen **pillar** to see over the walls.

'He's being held by Bandar,' Baloo said.

Kaa **slithered** her large body up and over the wall.

When they heard the **terrified** cries of the monkeys, Baloo and Bagheera followed.

**pillar** - *A tall, strong post that is used to hold up a building. It is usually made of bricks, stone or wood.*

**slithered** - *To slide, twist or curl in movement.*

**terrified** - *Very scared.*

The monkeys ran from Kaa and her **hypnotic** eyes. Baloo and Bagheera ran through the path that Kaa had cleared for them.

'Let Mowgli go or we'll let Kaa eat all of you!' said Baloo.

Bandar looked around, thinking. With a sigh and a **scowl**, he released Mowgli.

**hypnotic** - A sleepy feeling that often causes thoughts to be focussed on one thing. This is caused by another person or, in this case, animal.

**scowl** - An angry frown on a person's face.

'Don't think you've won, man cub,' said Bandar. 'Shere Khan is coming for you. He will get you!'

Bagheera and Baloo had already heard this news.

Mowgli would have to make a tough choice. He could stay and fight the tiger, or leave the jungle forever.

## Chapter 6

A few days later, Mowgli was playing with Grey when Father Wolf ran into the den.

'Have you heard?' shouted Father Wolf. 'Akela missed his **prey** when we were out hunting!'

Everyone looked worried. They all knew that if the pack leader missed their **prey**, they couldn't be the leader anymore.

**prey** - *An animal that is caught and killed for food by another animal.*

'What happens now?' Mother Wolf asked.

'The pack will need to find a new leader,' Father Wolf said.

'But we must be careful. The new leader may not want to protect Mowgli. Then he'll be in danger.'

That night, Father Wolf went to Council Rock. Bagheera listened from a nearby tree.

There was an **elderly** wolf where Akela usually stood.

'We must choose a new leader,' said the old wolf. 'Who has the strength to lead?'

None of the wolves spoke.

**elderly** - *Someone that is old.*

Father Wolf looked worried.

'What is happening?' Bagheera asked Father Wolf.

'No one wants to take Akela's place,' Father Wolf said. 'As soon as Shere Khan knows we don't have a leader, Mowgli will be in danger. He won't have the protection of the pack anymore.'

## Chapter 7

Mowgli did not leave the den for many days. Father Wolf stood outside of the cave in case Shere Khan appeared.

'Can I see Baloo?' Mowgli asked.

'No,' Mother Wolf said. 'Until the pack has a new leader, it isn't safe.'

'Quiet!' Father Wolf growled. 'Something is coming.'

Two wolves came out of the jungle.

Father Wolf growled, **baring his teeth**.

'We want the man cub,' said one of the wolves. 'If we give the boy to Shere Khan now, he will leave us alone.'

'You leave my cub alone!' Mother Wolf shouted.

**baring his teeth** - *Showing sharp teeth to scare someone during or before a possible fight.*

The two wolves left, but Mowgli was scared. The wolves were much stronger than him.

'Get Bagheera and Baloo,'
Mother Wolf told Father Wolf.
'We will need help protecting Mowgli.'

When Bagheera and Baloo arrived, they talked to Father Wolf and Mother Wolf outside. Mowgli waited in the cave and drew pictures on the cave walls.

After a while, Baloo called, 'Come outside, Mowgli!'

Mowgli went outside.

'We have decided to take you to the man village,' Mother Wolf said.

Mowgli was shocked. How could his family make him leave?

'I won't go!' Mowgli cried. 'You can't make me!'

Father Wolf told Mowgli that he had to go to the man village because they had fire. Shere Khan was afraid of fire, so Mowgli would be safe there.

'Baloo and I will take you to the man village,' Bagheera explained.

'Come on, kid,' said Baloo.

Mowgli began to cry. He did not want to leave his home, but he knew he had no choice.

He hugged his family, then left with Baloo and Bagheera.

As they walked, Mowgli tried to remember the path. He might need to get back to the wolf den one day.

Soon, they saw the man village on the other side of a river.

The village was **surrounded** by fire, and inside were people who looked like Mowgli.

'Fire will protect you,' said Bagheera. 'Shere Khan is afraid of it. If you stay inside the man village, you will be safe.'

**surrounded** - When something is all around.

## Chapter 8

Mowgli hugged Baloo and Bagheera, then walked towards the man village.

A man holding a torch of fire walked to Mowgli.

The man walked on two legs just like Mowgli. But Mowgli could not understand the man.

The man did not talk like the animals of the jungle.

Soon, a woman walked up to Mowgli, took his hand and **gestured** for him to follow her.

'I am Messua,' said the woman.

He followed the woman to her house made of mud.

**gestured** - *When someone or something uses their body, often their hands or head, to show what they mean.*

That night, Messua took Mowgli to the middle of the man village.

The middle of the village reminded Mowgli of Council Rock, but this time it wouldn't be Akela leading them, it would be an old man.

Everyone spoke about Mowgli and if he could stay in the man village.

After talking, the old man told Mowgli he could stay.

## Chapter 9

Mowgli missed Mother Wolf and his family, but he liked the man village.

Messua taught Mowgli the rules of the man village. Mowgli learnt to talk like the humans and wear the same clothes.

But Mowgli did not like his new bed. It was too soft for him.

One night, Mowgli went to the edge of the man village and saw Grey.

The two brothers hugged.

'I needed to see you,' said Grey. 'Shere Khan is trying to find you and is **threatening** everyone so they tell him where you are!'

**threatening** - *When someone says they are going to hurt someone else.*

After Grey left, Mowgli was worried that Shere Khan might hurt his family. But still, Mowgli stayed in the man village.

He helped the farmers by speaking to the buffalo using the Master Words he had learnt.

The other men were **jealous** because Mowgli could control the buffalo so well.

**jealous** - *When someone wants something that another person has.*

Grey would often visit Mowgli to tell him what was happening in the jungle.

One night, Grey did not visit Mowgli. Mowgli was worried that Shere Khan had hurt Grey.

But soon, Grey came back again.

'I'm sorry,' said Grey. 'I couldn't see you because the wolf pack are worried. Shere Khan is going to attack them unless they help him find you.'

Mowgli was angry because the tiger would not leave him alone.

'Stay safe, Mowgli,' said Grey, running back into the jungle.

## Chapter 10

That night, a group of angry men came to the house Mowgli was staying in.

'We saw him talking to a wolf!' one of the men shouted.

Mowgli knew they had seen him with Grey. But the men couldn't prove that they had seen Mowgli talking to Grey, so they walked away.

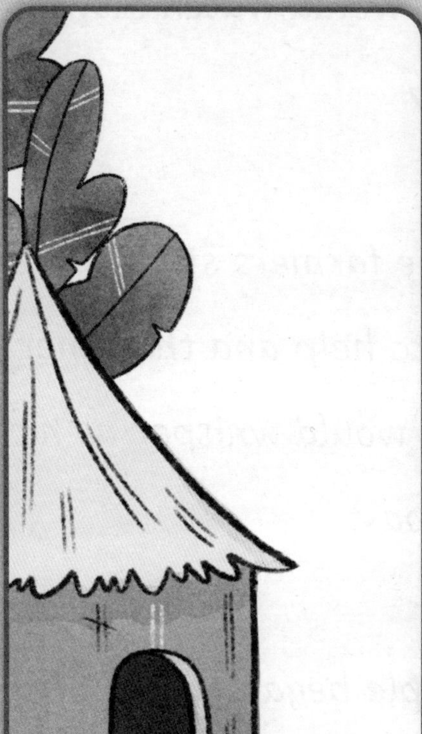

Every time Mowgli left the house, the men would watch Mowgli carefully.

Soon, the farmers stopped asking Mowgli to help and the other children would whisper as he walked past.

The people began to feel afraid of Mowgli.

Later that night, Mowgli couldn't sleep. He went to the jungle.

As he looked into the jungle, he saw a pair of eyes looking back at him. But it wasn't Grey.

It was Shere Khan!

The tiger came closer, but stopped when he saw the fire around the man village.

The next day, Mowgli made a torch with fire.

He was going to go back into the jungle to fight Shere Khan! Mowgli wanted to make Shere Khan leave him and the wolves alone.

The only thing Shere Khan was afraid of was fire. So Mowgli was going to bring fire with him!

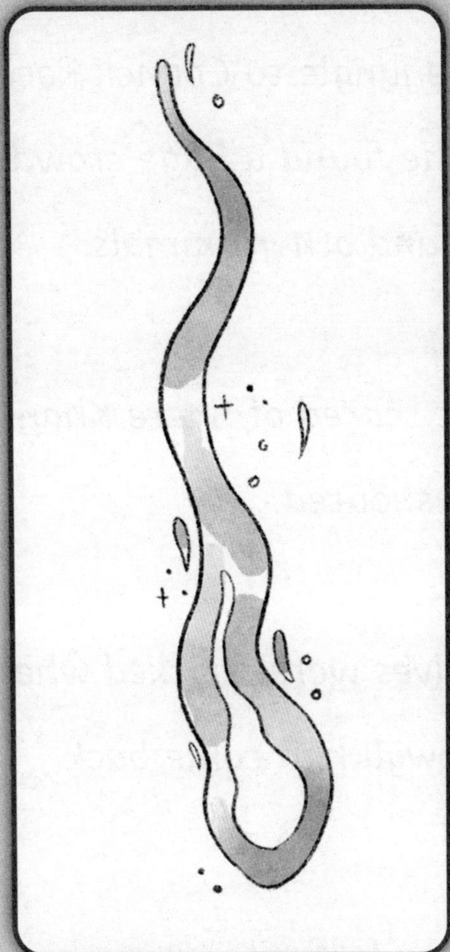

Mowgli followed the path back into the jungle to Council Rock. There, he found a huge crowd of wolves and other animals.

'I'm not scared of Shere Khan!' Mowgli shouted.

The wolves were shocked when they saw Mowgli had come back.

'Well, well, you are finally back,' came a voice from above. Mowgli looked up and saw Shere Khan in the tree above him.

Shere Khan jumped down. Father Wolf stood in front of Mowgli to protect him.

'You can't beat me in a fight,' Shere Khan said to Father Wolf.

Suddenly, Mowgli leapt forward, waving his torch of fire at Shere Khan.

Shere Khan jumped backwards and shouted, 'Keep that fire away from me!'

'Or what?' came a voice from behind Mowgli. It was Baloo!

Baloo came to stand behind Mowgli. Bagheera did too.

## Chapter 11

*Shere Khan bared his teeth as Father Wolf, Baloo and Bagheera surrounded him.*

*Shere Khan was about to attack, when Mowgli swung his torch and set fire to the tiger's tail!*

*'What have you done?' roared Shere Khan, trying to get away from the flame on his tail.*

Slowly, more wolves came forward to surround Shere Khan. The tiger became scared.

'Leave the jungle and never come back!' Mowgli shouted.

Terrified, Shere Khan turned and ran away into the jungle.

When Shere Khan had **disappeared**, Mowgli blew out his torch and hugged all of his friends and family.

Father Wolf said, 'I vote that Akela be our leader once more, with Mowgli by his side!'

The wolves howled to show they agreed.

**disappeared** - No longer able to be seen.

'We thought we were protecting you, Mowgli,' said Father Wolf. 'But really, you will protect us.'

Mowgli hugged Father Wolf knowing they would never be apart again.

*The End.*

## Rudyard Kipling

In 1865, Rudyard Kipling was born in Mumbai. Mumbai is a city in India.

Kipling and his parents came to England, but his parents left him in a foster home. After many years, he went back to India.

His poems and books became very popular. He wrote *The Jungle Book* in 1894.